LOOK AND FIND®

Disney

G·FORCE

© 2009 Disney Enterprises, Inc.
All Rights Reserved.

Adapted by Julia Lobo
Illustrated by Art Mawhinney

Based on the screenplay by The Wibberleys and
Ted Elliott & Terry Rossio and Tim Firth
Based on a story by Hoyt Yeatman
Executive Producers Mike Stenson, Chad Oman,
Duncan Henderson, David James
Produced by Jerry Bruckheimer
Directed by Hoyt Yeatman

Published by Louis Weber, C.E.O.
Publications International, Ltd.
7373 North Cicero Avenue
Lincolnwood, Illinois 60712
Ground Floor, 59 Gloucester Place
London W1U 8JJ

Customer Service: 1-800-595-8484 or
customer_service@pilbooks.com

www.pilbooks.com

Manufactured in China.

p i kids is a registered trademark
of Publications International, Ltd.
Look and Find is a
registered trademark
of Publications International, Ltd.,
in the United States and in Canada.

8 7 6 5 4 3 2 1

ISBN-13: 978-1-4127-9402-2
ISBN-10: 1-4127-9402-1

Is the billionaire inventor Leonard Saber developing sinister home appliances that are programmed to take over the world? To find out, the G-Force must infiltrate Saber's high-security mansion. Search the scene for the highly trained members of the G-Force.

Darwin

Speckles

Blaster

Juarez

Mooch

In the grand ballroom of his mansion, Leonard Saber unveils SaberSense, the newest technology from Saberling Industries. Mooch, the smallest member of the G-Force, obtains video surveillance of the event. Scout out these landing pads that Mooch will use for the job.

When they're not on a mission, the members of the G-Force make themselves at home in Ben's biological intelligence lab. Search in and around their apartments for these items that belong to Darwin, Juarez, Speckles, and Blaster.

NO PAIN
NO GAIN

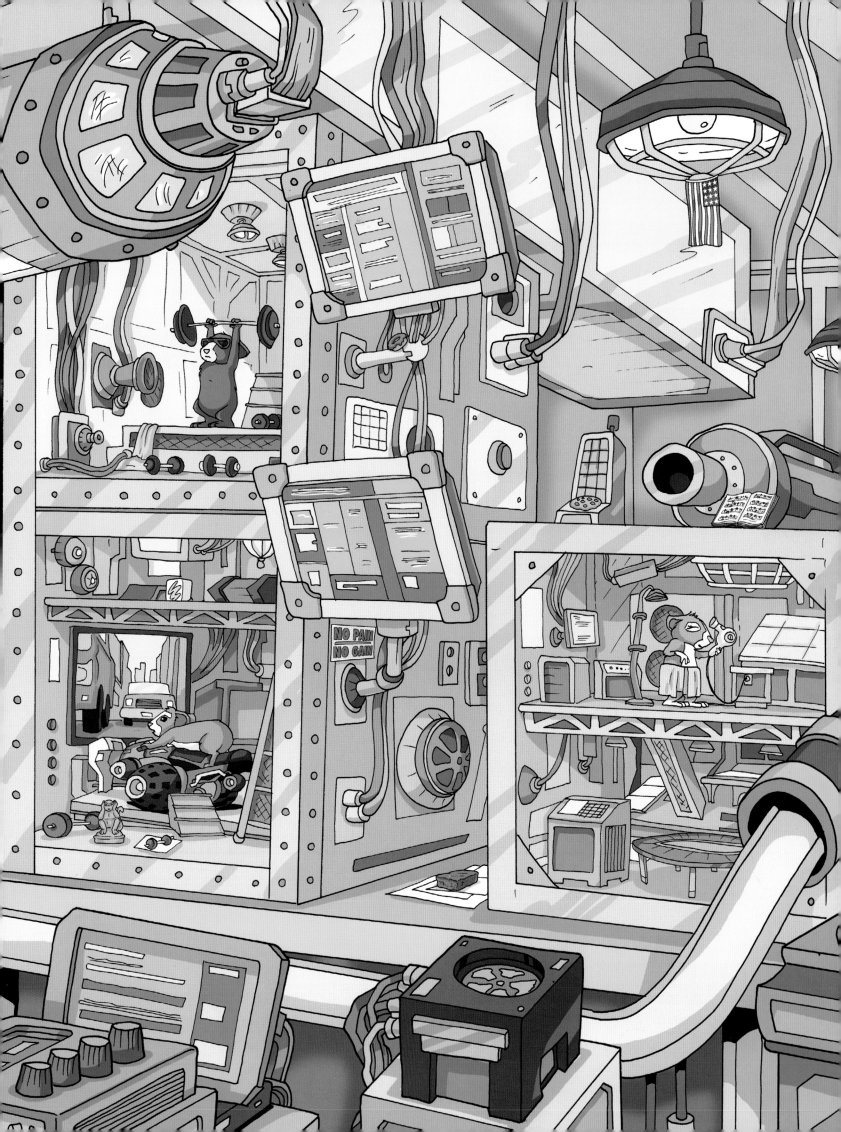

When the FBI decides to shut down Ben's lab, the G-Force has to make a break for it. Look for these supplies from Elia's Pet Shop that might make good hiding places until the coast is clear.

After hiding in a pet carrier, the team members find themselves in a strange environment—a pet store! Their new friend Hurley explains that people come there to buy pets. Look around Elia's Pet Shop to find these animals that are for sale.

The G-Force regroups at Ben's house only to be discovered by the FBI agents. To avoid capture, the team members speed off in the Rapid Deployment Vehicle that Ben designed for them. As they race across a parking lot, the agents' car sets off a fireworks show. Find these fireworks as they explode across the sky.

Across the country, Saberling appliances have turned into weapons. The SaberSense chips implanted deep within the machines draw them together to form powerful—and frightening—clusters. Search the scene to find these Saberling products that have gone on the attack!

The team members discover that one of their own is behind the plot, and only they can stop him! As the G-Force tries to defeat the Clusterstorm, search for these items from the Saber mansion.

As the team attempts to infiltrate Saber's mansion, they must evade detection by the security detail. Return to the mansion grounds to find these guards and guard dogs.

Saberling appliances and electronics are so popular you can find their logo in practically every home in the country. Return to the Saber mansion to find these items with the Saberling logo.

Fly back to Ben's bio lab to find these sweet treats that Mooch has hidden around the lab.

When the FBI shuts down Ben's lab, Ben's cockroaches also make a break for it. Return to the loading dock to find 10 cockroaches making their escape.

The animals in the pet shop don't have any high-tech gadgets. Hop back to the pet shop to find these low-tech toys.

Head back to the fireworks display to spot these spectators who are surprised to find that the show is starting a little bit early!

While the Saberling 5000 Series appliances go on the attack, giant magnets cause space debris to crash into the Earth. Search the street for these pieces of space junk.

Swing back to the battle scene to find the appliances that were marching down the street — and that are now part of the Clusterstorm!